FOR SHANK AND OTTO,
WITH LOVE


Printed in Hong Kong
Designed by Virginia Evans
Third printing

Library of Congress Cataloging-in-Publication Data
Paradis, Susan.
My Daddy / Susan Paradis.—1st ed.
p. cm.
Summary: A young boy marvels at the things his daddy can do including cross the street alone, run outside without a coat, stay up way past midnight, and wander in the deepest woods.
ISBN 1-886910-30-8 (alk. paper)
[1. Fathers—Fiction.] I. Title
PZ7.P2127Ms 1998
[E]—dc21 97-45857

# MY DADDY

SUSAN PARADIS

Front Street

ASHEVILLE, NORTH CAROLINA

1998

My daddy

can cross the

street alone.

He runs outside

without

a coat.

He is brave

enough to

mow the lawn

and ride

a big

two-wheeler.

He can dive

through

giant waves

and dig

a hole

to China.

My daddy can

touch his finger

to the moon

and stay up

way past

midnight.

His sneeze

is like

thunder

and his voice

can fill

the night.

He always finds

his way

back home.

Then

my daddy

hugs me

and spins

my world

around.

And when

my daddy

throws me high,

I fly . . .